Why goats don't make good lawn mowers

Caitlin pushed. She pulled. She wrapped her arms around the goat's neck and tried to nudge, prod, tug, and shove. It did no good. Salome stood there like a fat concrete statue. There was no stopping her as she bit off every lilac cluster she could reach.

"Don't, Salome! Please don't!" Caitlin begged. She might as well have asked the grass to stop growing.

Caitlin's Big Idea

by Gloria Skurzynski

illustrated by Cathy Diefendorf

little rainbow®
Troll

For Joni Alm,
who creates with
yarn, fabric, and love
—G. S.

Text copyright © 1995 by Gloria Skurzynski.

Illustrations copyright © 1995 by Troll Communications L.L.C.

Published by Little Rainbow, an imprint and trademark of
Troll Communications L.L.C.

Printed in the United States of America.

10 9 8 7 6 5 4 3 2

Library of Congress Cataloging-in-Publication Data

Skurzynski, Gloria.
Caitlin's big idea / by Gloria Skurzynski.
p.   cm.
Summary: Nine-year-old Caitlin is always trying to help her
neighbors, her friends and her mother, but the results often aren't
what she intends.
ISBN 0-8167-3814-9 (lib.)   ISBN 0-8167-3592-1 (pbk.)
[1. Helpfulness—Fiction.   2. Science projects—Fiction.
3. Mothers and daughters—Fiction.]   I. Title.
PZ7.S6287Cai   1995   [Fic]—dc20   94-27622

Contents

Mrs. Chesnut

A noise woke Caitlin, the noise of a motor. It couldn't be an airplane, she decided, because it didn't fade away. It didn't sound like her mother's old, beat-up car, either.

Caitlin got out of bed. Her room was the farthest back in the mobile home. To get outside, she had to cross through every other room, one after the other.

Through the bedroom, where her mother still slept, through the kitchen, through the living room, and out the front door Caitlin tiptoed, to find out what was making the noise.

The sun had already risen. It balanced on the north peak of the nearby mountain range like a ball on a seal's nose. The morning felt brand-new and fresh. It would have been perfect if it hadn't been so noisy.

"Hi, Mrs. Chesnut," she shouted to the woman in the trailer lot next door. Mrs. Chesnut didn't answer. She couldn't hear Caitlin over the noise her lawn mower was making. But the mower wasn't moving. It stood still, roaring away, right in the middle of Mrs. Chesnut's yard.

As Caitlin watched, Mrs. Chesnut grabbed the handles of the lawn mower. Then she let go as if she'd been stung. She shook her head and stamped her foot. She did the same thing again—clutched the handles, let go quickly, and stamped her foot, looking annoyed. Finally, she turned off the motor.

"Hi, Mrs. Chesnut," Caitlin called again. "What are you doing?"

"Nothing!" Mrs. Chesnut said, sounding exasperated. "Nothing at all. If you'd asked what I was trying to do, I'd tell you. I was trying to cut the grass. But I can't."

Slowly, stiffly, Mrs. Chesnut lowered herself onto the front steps of her mobile home. "My yard is a mess," she complained. "When my husband, Artie, was alive, we had the prettiest yard in the whole trailer court. Now it's awful. Just look!"

Although it was only May, the grass in Mrs. Chesnut's yard stood tall and straggly. Weeds poked through the blades of grass—spiky yellow dandelions, fuzzy tufts of burdock, and other wild-looking things Caitlin didn't know the names of.

"Your lilacs are beautiful, anyway," Caitlin said. In the morning light, Mrs. Chesnut's lilacs looked like bursts of cloud, all purple and lavender and pink.

Mrs. Chesnut smoothed her cotton housedress over her skinny knees. "Yes, the lilacs are the only pretty things I have left. The problem is, I can't push the lawn mower because I can't get a good grip on it. My arthritis hurts too bad." She held up her hands to show Caitlin her knobby knuckles. "And I can't afford to pay someone else to do it."

"I'll do it!" Caitlin offered. "You wouldn't have to pay me anything."

"Absolutely not! I'd never let a child touch a dangerous machine like that lawn mower. Why, Caitlin, you're only nine years old."

"I'm nearly ten," Caitlin argued. "In seven more months, I'll be ten all the way. I'm big enough to help."

"No one can help me, child," Mrs. Chesnut said sadly. "Old age is my problem, and there's nothing anyone can do about that."

"Cait-lin!" her mother called. "What are you doing outside in your pajamas? Come in and get ready for school."

"'Bye, Mrs. Chesnut. I'll try to think of a way to get your grass cut." Caitlin waved and then ran inside her mobile home.

Hats

"Mother, we have to do something for Mrs. Chesnut," Caitlin said. "I mean, *you* have to do something for her. She won't let me."

"Do what?" her mother asked.

"She needs her grass cut," Caitlin answered. "But she can't push her lawn mower because her arthritis hurts. So I think you should cut her grass for her."

"Oh, Caitlin, just look around here!" Her mother leaned against the living room wall and pointed to the mess.

Ski hats in rainbow colors lay strewn on the sofa. Chairs held more piles of Alpine ski hats and Nordic ski hats, each with a name knitted into the design. Since it was May, the names were mostly Spanish: *Juan, Myriam, Raul, José, Lalo, Rosa, Luis,* and others.

Caitlin's mother earned their living by making ski hats

on her knitting machine. In winter the hats were sold at the Three Peaks Ski Resort, ten miles east of Three Peaks Trailer Court, where they lived. At that time of year the names on the hats were more American, like *Brad* and *Chad* and *Heather, Tyler* and *Mark* and *Jill,* or *Mike, Kim,* and *Katie.*

When the winter ski season ended at Three Peaks, it was just beginning to be winter in the lower half of the world. Then Caitlin's mother sent her ski hats to South America, to resorts in Chile and Argentina. That was why the names she was now knitting on them were Spanish.

Caitlin had always found it hard to believe that summertime in North America was wintertime in South America. And vice versa. But her mother assured her that it was true.

"I was up till two-thirty last night working on this order of hats," her mother said now. "It has to be mailed the day after tomorrow. One hundred hats, and I only have sixty-three finished. I'll be up till two again tonight."

"So you can't cut Mrs. Chesnut's grass?" Caitlin asked.

"Honey, I just explained why I couldn't. Didn't you listen?"

Caitlin wound a scrap of yarn around her fingers. "She can't afford to pay someone to cut it."

Her mother answered, "If I don't get these hats mailed, you and I won't be able to afford to *eat.*"

Caitlin's mouth turned down at the corners. She knew

how hard her mother worked to buy them food and to pay the rent on their trailer space. Not to mention the cost of jeans and sweaters and shoes for Caitlin, and of gas for their old car.

"Speaking of food," her mother said, yawning around the words, "will you fix your own breakfast this morning and pack your lunch, so I can start knitting? I hard-boiled some eggs. They're in the fridge."

"Okay." Caitlin was glad there was something she could do to help her mother, who looked so tired. She wanted to help Mrs. Chesnut, too, if only she could think of a way.

CHAPTER 3

Salome

The school bus door swung open, and Mr. Billings, the driver, said, "Hurry. Hurry." He always said that.

Joe Daniel Giles jumped down first from the bus step. Caitlin jumped after him. They were the only two kids who got off at Three Peaks Trailer Court.

They walked together down the unpaved road to Joe Daniel's grandparents' ranch house. The Giles ranch covered a hundred acres of good grazing land, with Three Peaks Trailer Court taking up just a small space at one end. In winter the court's twelve lots were filled with the trailers of people who worked at the ski resort; when summer came, those people left for other jobs in other places. Only Caitlin, her mother, and Mrs. Chesnut lived at the trailer court all year round.

"Could you cut Mrs. Chesnut's grass this afternoon?" Caitlin asked Joe Daniel.

"Can't," he answered. "I have to do chores. Every day, I have to do chores."

"Don't you ever get to play?" she asked.

"Who's there to play with out here?"

"Me!" she wanted to shout, but she didn't. Joe Daniel was a sixth grader, and a sixth-grade boy couldn't— wouldn't!—ever play with a third-grade girl.

Sometimes, but only when no one else was around, Joe Daniel talked to Caitlin. Today he wasn't saying much, so she began to chatter, "See, Mrs. Chesnut has arthritis too bad to push the lawn mower. She used to have a husband to cut the grass, but he died. And now . . ."

Out of the blue, Joe Daniel asked, "What ever happened to your father?"

Surprised, Caitlin answered, "I don't know." In the three years they'd known each other, Joe Daniel had never asked her anything like that. "He left us when I was a baby," she said. "I don't even remember him."

"Does he ever send a postcard or anything?"

"No." Since Joe Daniel had brought up the subject, Caitlin decided to ask him a question, too. "What about your parents? Do they ever send you a postcard?"

"Don't be dumb." He looked disgusted with her. "How could they? They died when I was younger than you, even. Why do you think I live with my grand-parents?"

"You never told me," she mumbled. "I'm sorry."

"That's all right," he said. "At least I remember both my parents, so I'm luckier than you."

Was he? Caitlin had her mother. Was it better to have a mother and not remember your father who'd left you, or better to remember your parents but live with your grandparents? She wasn't sure.

They'd almost reached the ranch house. "I have to go in and change clothes," Joe Daniel said. "See you tomorrow on the bus."

"See you," Caitlin answered. She stood watching him walk all the way up the path to his back door. Then she scuffed her shoe soles toward the Giles's barn.

"Come here, cats," she called, but the Giles's barn cats wouldn't come near her. Barn cats were always skittery.

Caitlin longed to have a pet, but her mother was allergic to dog hair and cat hair, so they couldn't. Almost every day after school, Caitlin stopped at the Giles's barn, not to play with the cats, but to visit Salome, the goat. She'd known Salome since both of them were kids.

That was the correct name for a little goat—a kid.

Caitlin had fallen in love with Salome right from the start. When Salome was a newborn kid, Caitlin could pick her up and hold her. The baby goat would push her curly, hornless head against Caitlin's hand, to be rubbed. She'd felt so cuddly then, and she'd smelled so sweet.

Now Salome was a full-grown nanny goat, tethered to a tree outside the barn. "Hi, Salome," Caitlin said,

rubbing the goat's springy ears. Salome nodded in greeting and then went back to chewing grass.

"Your tether needs to be moved," Caitlin told her. "There's hardly any grass left. Wait, I'll get you some."

Caitlin pulled a handful of sweet, new grass and alfalfa from a spot outside Salome's reach. She loved to feel Salome's soft, gentle lips nibbling on her fingers.

The minute she picked up a second handful of grass, Caitlin got an idea.

CHAPTER

The Mower

"May I take Salome for a walk?" Caitlin asked Joe Daniel's grandfather, who was mucking out a horse stall in the barn.

Mr. Giles stopped working. He leaned on his pitchfork to stare at Caitlin. "I never heard of anyone taking a goat for a walk," he said.

"You know she follows me like a puppy," Caitlin coaxed. "I won't take her far. Just down to the trailer court and back."

Mr. Giles took off his cowboy hat. He wiped his forehead with his sleeve while he thought things over. Then he put the hat back on and said, "I guess it can't hurt anything if you lead her by the rope. But taking a goat for a walk—I never heard of such a thing."

"Thank you, Mr. Giles," Caitlin cried. "Don't worry, I'll take good care of her. I'll have her home by dinnertime."

"Goats eat dinner all day long," Mr. Giles muttered as he went back to cleaning the stall.

Caitlin hurried out of the barn and ran to where Salome stood tethered. "I have a big, important job for you," she explained as she untied the goat. "You won't even know it's a job. You'll think it's . . . dessert!"

After winding the end of the rope around her hand, Caitlin led Salome to the dirt road. Salome followed willingly. She began to trot, which made Caitlin trot, too, to keep up. In just ten minutes, they'd reached Mrs. Chesnut's trailer lot.

"Look what I brought you, Mrs. Chesnut," Caitlin called, but there was no answer. Then she remembered it was Wednesday, the day Mrs. Chesnut got a ride to the Senior Citizens' Center in Three Peaks.

"That's even better," she told Salome. "It'll be a surprise for her when she gets back." She looked at Salome, who looked back at Caitlin. How do you explain to a goat what you want her to do, Caitlin wondered.

"See, nice grass," she said. "Don't those dandelions look good? Eat, Salome! Mow Mrs. Chesnut's lawn with your teeth." Caitlin tried to push Salome's head down, but the goat wasn't interested. Instead, she stared straight ahead at the lilacs.

"No! Not those!" Caitlin yelled, but Salome had already snipped off a big purple lilac. Caitlin tugged the rope, which was tied to a collar around Salome's neck. Salome didn't budge, except for her jaws. They moved up and down and sideways as she enjoyed the treat.

"Salome, stop!" Caitlin screamed. Salome ate another spray of lilacs, and then another.

Caitlin pushed. She pulled. She wrapped her arms around the goat's neck and tried to nudge, prod, tug, and shove. It did no good. Salome stood there like a fat concrete statue. There was no stopping her as she bit off every lilac cluster she could reach.

Caitlin tried to push some of the lilacs out of the way, but the branches just sprang back to Salome's waiting teeth.

"Don't, Salome! Please don't!" Caitlin begged. She might as well have asked the grass to stop growing.

A car door slammed, and Mrs. Chesnut ran into the yard. "What is that animal doing here?" she yelled. "It's eating my lilacs!" she shrieked, answering her own question. "Stop that, goat! Caitlin, make it stop!"

Shouting, Mrs. Chesnut threw herself against Salome's side. Since Caitlin was already shouting and pushing from the other side, all they did was squeeze Salome's fat stomach. Salome *baaa'd,* dropping a cluster of lavender blooms.

The racket brought Caitlin's mother out of their mobile home. She started yelling, too—at Caitlin. "Pull the goat's head away from the bushes!" she cried.

"I'm trying to!" But Caitlin wasn't strong enough. Neither was Mrs. Chesnut. Caitlin's mother ran up to them and immediately started to sneeze. It seemed she was as allergic to goat hair as she was to dog and cat hair.

The sneezing didn't stop Caitlin's mother from taking charge. She grabbed the rope and wound it around Salome's snout. Astonished, Salome shook her head. She couldn't imagine why her mouth wouldn't open.

"Why did you bring that goat down here?" Caitlin's mother yelled, between sneezes.

"I thought she could eat Mrs. Chesnut's grass. Like a lawn mower. I didn't think she'd eat the lilacs!"

"You didn't think!" her mother shouted. "That's your problem, Caitlin—you never think things through. Now look what you've done!"

"My lilacs," Mrs. Chesnut mourned. "My beautiful lilacs! They were the only nice things in my yard."

Salome wagged her head hard to shake the rope off her snout. When she couldn't get it loose, she became alarmed and bolted out of the yard. Up the dirt road she ran, toward her home barn.

"Wait for me!" Caitlin cried, running after her. With each gallop of Salome's hooves, the rope loosened. Caitlin caught up and finished unwinding it just as they reached the barn. She skidded to a stop in front of Mr. Giles.

"Have a nice walk?" he asked. "You must have run instead of walked. You and the goat are both panting."

Caitlin didn't have enough breath to answer. She just nodded to Mr. Giles before she turned to go home.

""Darnedest thing," he muttered as he watched Caitlin scuff down the road. "Never heard of taking a goat for a walk!"

CHAPTER 5

Trouble

Caitlin woke up early the next morning. Lying in bed, she thought about how much trouble she'd caused. Her mother had finally forgiven her, but Caitlin didn't know whether Mrs. Chesnut would ever speak to her again.

Her mother was already up and working at the knitting machine. "Honey, would you mind fixing your own breakfast again today?" she asked when Caitlin appeared. "And pack your lunch, too. I'm sorry you have to do it two days in a row, but I just don't have time." She stopped knitting to rub her eyes. "I've been up most of the night trying to finish these hats."

"Sure, Mom," Caitlin said, feeling bad all over again that she'd been such a troublemaker. Between spoonfuls of cereal, she put an apple, two hard-boiled eggs, and a wheat roll into her lunch box.

From the doorway she blew her mother a kiss and then

turned and trudged up the hill. It was far too early for the school bus, but Caitlin didn't care. The earlier she greeted a new morning, the better she liked it.

At the highway she climbed onto the wood-rail fence and sat facing three tall mountain peaks. North Peak, Middle Peak, and South Peak—those were the three peaks that gave the town, the school, the ski resort, and the trailer court their names.

She loved to watch the sun climb over the peaks. In the spring, the sun would always be up before she caught the school bus. At that time of year, it rose straight above North Peak, seeming to balance in the clouds at the tip of the peak.

Each week the morning sun moved a little farther north until just past the middle of June, when it would start traveling south again. Right around Christmas every year, it rose above South Peak.

Caitlin stopped admiring the sunrise to watch Joe Daniel walk toward her. He climbed onto the fence, letting his backpack dangle between his knees.

"I heard you got in trouble yesterday," he said.

Caitlin's stomach squeezed hard. If Joe Daniel knew about it, did everyone else know, too?

"How'd you find out?" she asked.

"Grandpa saw some lilac petals stuck on Salome's mouth. Mrs. Chesnut has the only lilacs around here, so Grandpa called her on the telephone. She told him what Salome did."

"Is she still mad at me?" Caitlin asked. "Mrs. Chesnut, I mean."

"Don't know. Here comes the bus."

Joe Daniel got on ahead of her and went to sit with the big boys in the back. Just once, Caitlin wished he'd sit with her. Just once. She knew better than to expect that, though. A sixth-grade boy would rather stand the whole way than sit with a third-grade girl. Especially a third-grade girl who got into trouble.

When they reached Three Peaks Elementary, Caitlin went straight to her homeroom. She stuffed her sweater and her lunch box inside her desk, and then folded her hands on the desk top. From now on, she intended to stay out of trouble. It was embarrassing to have someone like Joe Daniel know all about it when Caitlin did something dumb. No more, she promised herself.

"Good morning, girls and boys," the teacher said.

"Good morning, Miss Meese," they answered.

"I just want to remind you," Miss Meese said, "that tomorrow your science projects are due. You've had a whole month to prepare them, so I know you're going to bring in some wonderful work."

Caitlin's stomach clenched again. Harder, this time.

"The three best projects from each class will be entered in the state science fair," Miss Meese added.

The best projects! Caitlin wasn't worried about being best—she just needed *something* to turn in. She'd

forgotten all about the assignment. She needed more than a project. She needed an idea. Fast.

"As I'm sure you all remember," Miss Meese went on, "your project may be an experiment, a model, or an oral report."

Kevin Running Fox raised his hand to ask, "What's an oral report?"

"It's when you stand up and talk about your project." Miss Meese squinted her eyes at Kevin. "Does that question mean, Kevin, that you haven't even started on your project?"

While Kevin stammered, Caitlin slid down in her seat.

"I . . . hope . . . it . . . doesn't . . . mean . . . that!" Miss Meese said, stabbing the whole class, row by row, with her stare. "I would hate to think that *any one of you* will go home tonight and say, 'Mother, Dad, I need a science project for tomorrow.'"

Caitlin put her head down on her folded arms.

"You've known about this assignment for a whole month," Miss Meese reminded them. "Remember, it's against the rules for anyone to help you. You must do all the work by yourself. Tomorrow I expect to see some real excellence here. Now, please rise to say the Pledge of Allegiance."

Caitlin stood up with the others, but no words came out of her mouth. No one noticed that she was too upset to remember the Pledge of Allegiance. Tomorrow, though, everyone would know that she'd forgotten to do a science project.

Trouble. Again.

Help

After she got off the school bus, Caitlin went straight home for two reasons. First, she didn't want to run into Mr. Giles, since he knew about Salome. Second, she had to think up something for a science project.

In the front room Caitlin found the sofa completely covered with ski hats. They made splashes of bright color on the vinyl upholstery. On top of the hats lay Caitlin's mother, sound asleep.

"Poor Mom," Caitlin thought. "She's so tired. I wonder how many more hats she needs to make."

Caitlin looked at the knitting machine, where an unfinished hat hung on the needles. Her mother must have become so sleepy in the middle of knitting that she'd just had to lie down for a nap. Caitlin touched the machine needles. They looked like a hundred crochet hooks sticking out in a row, side by side.

Strands of pink and aqua yarn stretched from big

spools to the half-finished hat. Those colors would be for a woman or a girl. A pattern for the name had already been rolled into the machine. *Maria.* What a pretty name, she thought. In South America, where it would be winter now, an unknown Maria would soon ski down the slopes wearing the pink-and-aqua hat.

Caitlin had watched her mother make hundreds of hats. It was easy to do on a knitting machine. Caitlin touched the carriage handle with one finger, then wrapped her hand around it and slowly slid the carriage across the needles.

She'd knitted a row. By herself! Maybe she could finish the whole hat. Wouldn't her mother be surprised to wake up and find the hat all made?

Caitlin zipped the carriage back from left to right. All the needles seemed to be in the right place to begin knitting the first letter, the *M,* in pink.

Carefully, she moved the carriage from right to left again. Something was wrong. The needles that formed the letter *M* had moved into place, but the pink yarn hadn't. So the pink *M* hadn't begun. No pink showed at all.

Then she remembered. She hadn't pushed the special button to start a second color. Now what, she wondered. What would her mother do if that happened? She tried to remember.

First she tried to push the needles back to where they'd been before she'd moved the carriage. But she pushed them too far, and the yarn slipped off.

Now dozens of stitches had dropped. It wouldn't have

been so bad if all Caitlin had lost was the first row she'd done herself. But this looked a lot worse than that. Instead of the smoothly knitted edge she'd found when she came home from school, she was looking at a raggedy line of loops and squiggles.

Caitlin got up from her chair and tiptoed to the sofa. Bending over, she stared at her mother's eyelids. They didn't flutter. Her mother was still sound asleep.

Should she wake her? No, she'd better just try to fix the mess she'd made herself. She'd often watched her mother pick up dropped stitches to put them back on the needles. There was a special tool for it.

When Caitlin found the tool and lifted the first dropped stitch, the one next to it started to run. It ran just like a hole in panty hose. Each time she tried to pick up a stitch, other stitches ran.

"Oh, no!" she said aloud. The words just slipped out without her wanting them to.

"Caitlin, what are you doing?" her mother asked, sitting up on the sofa. Then she jumped to her feet and said the same thing, much louder. *"What are you doing!"*

Caitlin answered so softly she could hardly hear herself. "Helping," she said.

With one leap her mother reached the machine. "Helping! Haven't I told you never to touch my knitting machine?"

"I know, but . . ."

"*But!* I don't want to hear any *buts*! I'm tired of your excuses. I'm tired of you doing things you're not supposed to do. I'm tired of you getting into trouble. I'm just plain tired!" Her mother's voice, which had started out sounding so angry, now sounded like she was going to cry.

"I'm sorry," Caitlin wailed. "I didn't think I'd mess up your machine!"

"That's your trouble, Caitlin," her mother scolded. "You never think of the consequences. The next time you want to help someone, *Think,* Caitlin! *Think!*"

CHAPTER 7

The World in a Bonnet

After an hour, Caitlin's mother forgave her. That's how long it took her to unwind the yarn of the half-finished hat and start it all over again, from the beginning. At the end of the hour, the *Maria* hat was done.

For dinner they opened a can of ravioli. "That's your punishment for messing with my knitting machine," her mother said. "Canned ravioli. I was planning to make meat loaf tonight."

Meat loaf happened to be Caitlin's favorite dinner. Not having it was real punishment, but she understood the justice in that. The time her mother might have spent making meat loaf was used instead to redo the *Maria* hat.

Now dinner was over, and both of them were hard at work. Her mother sat at the machine, knitting a hat that read *Jorge*—for a man, or a boy, in South America. Caitlin had begun her science project.

First, she blew up a balloon and tied the end so the air wouldn't escape. Next, she tore newspaper into strips. After dampening the strips in a mixture of flour and water, she laid them over the balloon.

"What are you making?" her mother asked.

"My science project."

"What's it going to be?"

"The earth," Caitlin answered. "After I get these strips piled thick enough, I'll paint the oceans and continents on it." She had an almost-new box of water-colors, and she could copy the continents from the pictures in their atlas.

"That's nice," her mother murmured, intent on changing a spool of yarn from light blue to dark blue.

A while later, her mother asked, "When does your science project have to be turned in?"

"Tomorrow."

"Tomorrow!" Her mother whirled on her chair. "That papier-mâché will never dry in time. You can't paint it till it's dry."

"I know," Caitlin answered. "I'm going to dry it with the hair dryer."

"Good luck," her mother said, and went back to her knitting.

Caitlin was pleased with the way her sphere turned out. The thick flour-and-water paste stuck the paper to the balloon just right.

She plugged in the hair dryer and blasted hot air onto her project. After a few minutes, she turned off the dryer and felt her globe. It was still wet and sticky.

Sighing, Caitlin turned on the dryer again. The next time she checked, one small part of the globe seemed a little less damp than the rest. What she was doing would probably work, but it was going to take a long time.

After half an hour, Caitlin's arms ached. She tried holding the dryer in her left hand, but her left arm got too tired, so she switched back to her right. Slowly, the globe was drying. Very, very slowly. Caitlin's arms were growing weary much faster than the globe was getting dry.

"There's got to be an easier way," she told herself. After unplugging the dryer, she went to the closet in her mother's bedroom. That was the biggest closet in the mobile home, so they used it to store extra things—old things that weren't quite worn out enough to throw away.

Rummaging around, Caitlin finally found what she was looking for. Her mother was so busy working—she was doing a *Rubén* hat now—that she didn't pay attention when Caitlin came back.

Later, her mother said, "One more hat finished," and turned around. She seemed surprised to find Caitlin sitting on the floor, studying the picture of the world in the atlas.

"I thought you were drying your papier-mâché," her mother said. "I can still hear the hair dryer."

Caitlin pointed to the corner. From the storage closet,

she'd taken her mother's old, bonnet-style hair dryer. The bonnet, all puffed with hot air, sat on top of the world, blowing up a storm.

Her mother started to laugh, the first laughter Caitlin had heard from her in days. "Oh, Caitlin, that's wonderful!" she exclaimed. "That's using your head!"

"It's almost dry enough to paint," Caitlin told her. "I've been looking at South America, where you're going to send all those hats. Why is it winter there now, Mom?"

Her mother stretched her arms high above her head, yawned, and said, "It's kind of complicated. It would take me a few minutes to explain . . . but . . . Oh well, I could use a break."

Sitting on the floor next to Caitlin, her mother flipped through some pages of the atlas. "Look, here's the sun, and there's the earth," she said, and went on to explain to Caitlin why it was almost winter in South America but almost summer in Three Peaks.

Impressed, Caitlin asked, "How did you learn all that?"

"In school. I went to school once, you know. To college, for awhile. I wanted to be a teacher, but then . . . you came along." Her mother shrugged. "So I make hats instead."

Caitlin thought about that while her mother went back to sewing the seam of the brown-and-gold *Rubén* hat. "Did it make you angry?" she asked. "I mean, when I came along and you couldn't be a teacher. Did it make you mad that you had to knit hats instead?"

"Do you mean, am I the Mad Hatter?" Her mother laughed at her own joke. "Of course not. I'm glad I have you, Caitlin."

"Even when I do dumb things? Awful things?"

"Always. Every day, every minute, every second. I'm glad I have you."

Caitlin began to paint. She put a wide, happy smile on the world, in blue. Then she covered it up with the Pacific Ocean.

CHAPTER 8

Joe Daniel

The sun stood well above North Peak, but clouds hid most of the sun, and the mountaintop, too. A gusty wind blew, bouncing tumbleweeds along the highway.

Caitlin settled on the wood-rail fence to wait for the school bus. She hung her lunch box over a post and opened the plastic bag to take another look at her project. Since it was so windy, she didn't want to take it out of the bag. It might blow away.

Her earth looked beautiful. It was still damp in some spots, but the watercolors hadn't run or smeared, not a bit. When she saw Joe Daniel coming, she squeezed the bag shut so he couldn't see inside. He might think her project wasn't all that great. After all, he was a sixth grader.

"What's that stuff you're carrying?" she asked when he got close.

"A coconut." He held it out. "Haven't you ever seen one before?"

"Sure. In the supermarket," she said. "What's in your other hand?"

"A jar with a dandelion growing in it."

"What for?"

"My science project. It's about seed dispersal."

"What does that mean?" Caitlin asked.

"It means how seeds move around. To start new plants. A coconut can float—sometimes across oceans. You know about dandelions. They blow." Joe Daniel sat on the lower rail of the fence. He set the coconut and the jar on the ground.

Caitlin scrambled down to sit beside him. "That's really great," she said.

"I've got lots more specimens in my backpack," he told her. "I want to get picked for the state science fair."

"Can I see the rest of the stuff?" Caitlin asked.

"I don't know. It's pretty windy. I don't want any of it to blow away."

"You could hold it—I won't touch a thing," she promised. It would be exciting to see Joe Daniel's project before he took it to school.

"Okay, I'll open my backpack, and you can look inside. But swear you won't touch anything."

"I swear." She raised her right hand.

He lifted the flap of his pack and pointed. "That one's

a maple seed." It was glued to a paper with writing on it. Caitlin wished she could see better, but the flap got in the way.

"Maple seeds have wings that make them fly," Joe Daniel explained. "The next one's a thistle. It gets carried around when it sticks to someone's clothes."

Caitlin was enormously impressed.

"I've got pine nuts and tumbleweed and cotton from cottonwood trees," Joe Daniel said. "Twenty-two different specimens. Hey, here comes the bus."

The yellow bus pulled beside them, and the doors swung open. "Hurry, hurry," said Mr. Billings.

Joe Daniel stood up and then bent to get the coconut and the dandelion jar.

"I'll bring your backpack," Caitlin offered. She put her lunch box and her plastic bag into her left hand so she could reach with the backpack with her right.

"Hurry, hurry," Mr. Billings said.

Hurrying, Caitlin lifted Joe Daniel's backpack—*upside down!* The project papers all fell out, and the wind began to pick them up. They skipped and swirled down the highway. Others blew into sagebrush bushes along the road or got whisked high, high into the electric power lines.

"My project!" Joe Daniel yelled.

"I'll get them!" Caitlin screamed. While Joe Daniel grabbed for the papers on the ground, Caitlin scrambled after the ones blowing farther and farther away.

Mr. Billings leaned on the horn of the bus in a long, loud blast. Then he climbed down the bus steps and shouted, "Caitlin, get yourself back here! You can't go running around the highway."

"The papers!" Caitlin begged. "I have to . . ."

"Hang the papers!" Mr. Billings exploded. "I'm responsible for your safety. Get yourself on this bus right now! You, too, Joe Daniel."

She'd been able to catch only one paper, one with a juniper berry taped on it. Miserable, hanging her head, Caitlin got on the bus and sat in an empty seat.

Behind her, Joe Daniel climbed aboard, still stuffing papers into his backpack. His cheeks showed splotches of angry red. Wind had blown his hair into spikes that looked angry, too.

Joe Daniel headed for the back where the big boys sat, but Mr. Billings ordered him, "Sit down right there, next to Caitlin. You've wasted enough of my time."

Joe Daniel's eyes narrowed to slits and his lips tightened with fury as he hissed at Caitlin, "You've ruined my project. You are a walking disaster!"

The thing she'd wanted to happen for so long had happened at last—Joe Daniel was sitting beside her on the bus. Only he sat with his back to her, not talking, not looking at her, stiff with anger. He hated her!

His backpack lay on the seat between them. Not knowing what else she could do to make things up to Joe

Daniel, Caitlin took the earth out of her plastic bag. Carefully, so he wouldn't notice, she opened his pack and put her science project inside. It couldn't make up for what she'd done, but it was all she had to offer him.

CHAPTER 9

Seasons

"We'll start with the first person in the first row," Miss Meese said. "Lily, please come to the front of the room and demonstrate your science project."

Looking proud, Lily Kato showed the class a piece of dinosaur bone. It was real dinosaur bone, but over the past few million years it had turned to stone. Then Lily held up a fresh beef bone and told the class about the many ways it was like the dinosaur bone.

Caitlin didn't pay much attention to what Lily was saying. Instead, she counted the rows and the seats. Seventeen pupils and three more rows remained before it would be her turn.

What would she do? She didn't have a science project now.

Would Miss Meese send a note home with her, complaining that Caitlin hadn't done her homework? Her mother had seen her making the papier-mâché earth. She'd want to know what had happened to it.

Caitlin would have to explain that she'd given it to Joe Daniel. Her mother would want to know why.

She'd gotten into trouble on Wednesday, taking Salome to mow Mrs. Chesnut's grass.

She'd gotten into trouble on Thursday, trying to knit on her mother's machine.

She couldn't bear to have her mother find out that she'd gotten into trouble on Friday, too.

"Don't you ever think before you do these things?" her mother would ask. "Think, Caitlin! From now on, use your head!"

Kevin Running Fox stood in front of the class, explaining how his ancestors had made arrowheads. He showed them two arrowheads, but mostly he gave an oral report.

Quietly, Caitlin raised the lid of her desk. Was there anything inside she could talk about for an oral report? Nothing but her schoolbooks, a pile of papers, two pencils, a plastic case that held ten different-colored felt-tip pens, and her lunch box.

With her chin on her hands, Caitlin pretended to watch Emily Riddle's experiment. Emily held up two real teeth. They must have been her baby molars. One, bright and shiny, sat in a water glass. The other, all stained, lay at the bottom of an empty cola bottle. Emily said the clean tooth had been soaked in water and the grungy tooth in cola for a whole month, which proved it was better to drink water.

Caitlin lifted her desk lid again, hoping she'd missed something the first time. She opened her lunch box. Her mother had packed a big orange, two hard-boiled eggs, some chips, and a cookie.

Slowly, so that no one would notice what she was doing, she took out one of the eggs and set it in her lap. Then she opened the pack of felt-tip pens.

She squeezed her eyes tightly to help her remember. How had the earth looked when she'd painted it the night before? Keeping it small, she outlined North America on the egg with the brown pen. She used both brown and green to fill it in.

Beneath that, she drew South America. With blue, she colored the Atlantic Ocean. On the other side of the egg, Europe above, Africa below. Then Asia, above Australia. She left the bottom white for Antarctica, and filled in blue for the Pacific Ocean.

"Caitlin, your turn," Miss Meese said, just as Caitlin finished coloring the egg.

On her way to the front of the room, Caitlin asked Emily, "May I borrow your cola bottle? Only, take the tooth out first."

"Okay," said Emily.

Carrying her orange, the egg, and the empty cola

bottle, Caitlin walked to the front of the room. Everyone watched her. She could tell that they were wondering what she was going to do.

She stood the bottle on Miss Meese's desk. Carefully, she balanced the orange on the mouth of the bottle.

"That's the sun," she told them.

Lily Kato giggled, but no one else did.

"This," Caitlin said, lifting the hard-boiled egg, "is the earth. Everyone knows the earth goes around the sun. It takes a whole year to go all the way around once." She moved the egg around the orange to demonstrate.

"But the earth doesn't stand straight up," she went on. "It tilts a little, like this," and she showed them.

Miss Meese smiled and nodded.

Encouraged, Caitlin said, "When the top half of the earth—that's where we live—is tilted toward the sun, it's summer." She pointed to the continent of North America she'd drawn, which tipped toward the orange. "Like now, when it's almost summer here at Three Peaks."

The kids looked interested.

"Because of the tilt," Caitlin continued, "the bottom half of the earth is farther from the sun. That makes it winter down there. Right now, people are skiing in South America. I know, because my mother makes hats for them."

"Is that true?" Kevin Running Fox asked.

"Absolutely true," Miss Meese said.

"Why does it happen like that?" asked Kevin.

"Because," Caitlin answered, "when our part of the earth leans toward the sun, the sun's rays hit us straighter. So they're hotter. The rays have to slant more to reach the bottom part of the earth, so they're not as hot. It's like . . ."

Caitlin paused, trying to remember what her mother had talked about the evening before. "Like, at noon, when the sun beats straight down on you, it feels hottest. At sunrise and sunset, when it shines on you at a slant, it feels cooler."

As she explained it to the class, the whole thing became clearer to Caitlin, and she grew excited. "If the egg—I mean the earth—was straight up and down, the rays would always stay the same. There wouldn't be any different seasons. The tilt makes the seasons." She circled the orange with the egg again.

Caitlin's eyes got wide. "I just thought of something else. Is that why, in winter, the sun comes up over South Peak, but in summer, it comes up over North Peak?"

"Huh? I don't get it," Emily said.

"Everything fits together, but it's hard to understand at first," Miss Meese told them. "Caitlin, do more work on that part of it, would you? We need to move on to the next student now, but we'll call you back on Monday for a further report. That was an imaginative way to show us a difficult concept. Very good."

Caitlin's knees shook all the way back to her desk. It had gone pretty well! Now Miss Meese wouldn't send a note home. And Caitlin had the whole weekend to improve her project. Maybe she could use a grapefruit for the sun. No, a big yellow balloon! Or even better, something that could really shine, like a flashlight, or a lamp. She would paint another papier-mâché earth. . . .

"Oh, Caitlin," Miss Meese called, "would you mind missing recess? I'd like to talk to you."

Uh, oh, Caitlin thought. What now?

Good Thinking

Joe Daniel wasn't on the bus going home. Caitlin felt too shy to ask the big boys in the back what had happened to him. She tried to ask Mr. Billings after the bus reached her stop, but he only said, "Hurry. Hurry." Mr. Billings never wasted time talking.

Caitlin was glad to hurry all the way home. She couldn't wait to tell her mother the good news. As she skipped down the dirt road, coming closer to their trailer space, she heard a familiar noise. A motor.

Mrs. Chesnut sat on the steps of her mobile home, looking happy. It was easy to see what made her happy. Joe Daniel's grandfather, Mr. Giles, was pushing the lawn mower, cutting Mrs. Chesnut's grass.

"Your mother isn't home," Mrs. Chesnut shouted over the noise. "She asked me to tell you she'll be back real soon." Mrs. Chesnut patted the steps beside her, and Caitlin sat down.

Caitlin wanted to ask why Mr. Giles was cutting Mrs. Chesnut's grass. She had to yell to be heard. *"Why is . . ."* she began. When she got to *"Mr. Giles . . ."* he suddenly turned off the lawn mower.

"What do you want, Caitlin?" he asked. "Why'd you yell my name so loud? I'm not hard of hearing, you know."

"Sorry," she said, feeling silly. "I just wondered . . ."

"Why I'm here?" he finished for her. "Because of you. When I heard what you did with Salome, trying to get her to trim Mrs. Chesnut's yard, I felt kind of ashamed. I didn't know Mrs. Chesnut couldn't cut her grass anymore. Never thought about it. So I came to do it for her."

"So kind of Mr. Giles," the old woman murmured.

"Got to take care of my most faithful renter," he told her. "You've lived here longer than anyone else."

Not far away, at the top of a little hill in the dirt road, Joe Daniel appeared. He was running.

"Grandpa!" he called when he got closer. "Guess what!"

"Can't guess," Mr. Giles said. "Slow down and tell me."

After he reached them, Joe Daniel had to swallow to catch his breath.

"Why weren't you on the bus?" Caitlin asked.

"My science teacher gave me a ride home," he explained between deep breaths. "Grandpa, you know that science project I worked on? It got picked for the state science fair!"

"Wonderful!" Mr. Giles exclaimed.

"How? . . ." Caitlin began, but she stopped before she asked it aloud. How could Joe Daniel's project have been chosen when part of it had blown away?

He knew what she was wondering. "Only seven pages got lost," he told her. "I had fifteen specimens left. That was enough!"

A cloud of dust rose on the dirt road, and Caitlin's mother drove up in her old, beat-up car.

"The hats are finally in the mail," she said as she got out of the car. "What's happening here?"

Grinning, Mr. Giles told her, "Joe Daniel's project got picked for the state science fair." He put his arm around Joe Daniel. "This is one smart boy here. My grandson."

Caitlin thought how lucky Joe Daniel was to have such a nice grandfather. And how lucky she was to have her mother. Softly, she said, "My project got picked, too."

"How? . . ." Joe Daniel began, but stopped in time.

Caitlin knew what he meant—how could her project have been chosen when she'd put it into his backpack?

"Tell you later," she murmured. No one else heard, because they were all busy congratulating her—Mrs. Chesnut, Mr. Giles, and her mother.

"Someone will have to drive us to the science fair," Joe Daniel told them. "It'll be pretty far away, in the state capitol building."

"I'll drive the kids," Caitlin's mother offered.

"Mrs. Giles and I will want to go, too," Mr. Giles said.

"Why don't we all go together in my truck? The kids can ride in the back."

To ride with Joe Daniel in the back of a pickup truck— just the two of them! That would be a million times better than sitting next to him on the bus. "Except," Caitlin said, "we'd better keep the projects in the front of the truck. We wouldn't want them to blow away."

"Good thinking," said Mr. Giles.

Her mother gave Caitlin a big hug and whispered in her ear, "I am so proud of you. You're the greatest daughter under the sun."

Caitlin smiled. Her mother couldn't have said it any better, she thought.

Caitlin's
Monday Morning Report

Seasons
Around the World
The earth goes around
the sun once a year.
The earth also spins
like a top, all the way
around once every twenty-
four hours.
Half the earth is

turned toward the sun. That makes it daylight. Half the earth is turned away from the sun. That makes it dark. The edge between dark and light is where we see the sun rise. Every minute, the sun is rising somewhere on the earth.

This drawing will show why the sun rises over North Peak in the summer and over South Peak in the winter. The tilt makes it happen.

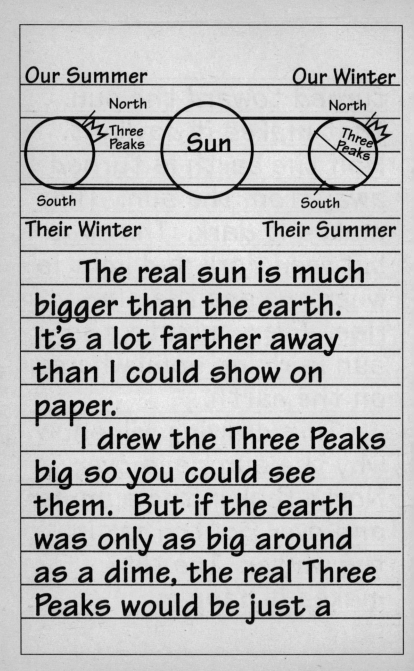

Our Summer   Our Winter

North   North

Three Peaks   Sun   Three Peaks

South   South

Their Winter   Their Summer

The real sun is much bigger than the earth. It's a lot farther away than I could show on paper.

I drew the Three Peaks big so you could see them. But if the earth was only as big around as a dime, the real Three Peaks would be just a

speck, smaller than a
pinpoint.

P.S. My mother showed
me how to trace around
a quarter for the sun
and around a dime for
the earth. But I did it
myself.

Look for these other books from

little rainbow®

THE BIRTHDAY WISH MYSTERY
by Faye Couch Reeves
illustrated by Marilyn Mets
0-8167-3531-X $2.95 U.S. / $3.95 Can.

MICE TO THE RESCUE
by Michelle V. Dionetti
illustrated by Carol Newsom
0-8167-3515-8 $2.95 U.S. / $3.95 Can.

THREE DOLLAR MULE
by Clyde Robert Bulla
illustrated by Paul Lantz
0-8167-3598-0 $2.50 U.S. / $3.50 Can.

THE WORLD'S GREATEST TOE SHOW
by Nancy Lamb and Muff Singer
illustrated by Blanche Sims
0-8167-3323-6 $2.50 U.S. / $3.50 Can.

NORMAN NEWMAN:
MY SISTER THE WITCH
by Ellen Conford
illustrated by Tim Jacobus
0-8167-3623-5 $2.50 U.S. / $3.50 Can.

Available wherever you buy books.